THE UNICORN'S SECRET

#7

Castle Avamir

D0089972

by Kathleen Duey
illustrated by Omar Rayyan

ALADDIN PAPERBACKS

New York   London   Toronto   Sydney

For all the daydreamers . . .

First Aladdin Paperbacks edition August 2003

Text copyright © 2003 by Kathleen Duey
Illustrations copyright © 2003 by Omar Rayyan

ALADDIN PAPERBACKS
An imprint of Simon & Schuster
Children's Publishing Division
1230 Avenue of the Americas
New York, NY 10020

Also available in an Aladdin Library edition.
Designed by Debra Sfetsios
The text of this book was set in Golden Cockerel ITC.

Printed in the United States of America
8 10 9
ISBN-13: 978-0-689-85372-2 (ISBN-10: 0-689-85372-6)

The Library of Congress Control Number for the Library Edition is 2003102697

0711 OFF

✦

The Gypsies have struggled over the wintry High Road into Lord Levin's lands. Spring rains are finally melting the snow. Moonsilver and Heart walk apart from the Gypsies. Strangers think Moonsilver is a lord's mount because of the fancy armor that hides his horn. In every village, every town, Heart asks about Castle Avamir. No one has ever heard of it.

✦

✦CHAPTER ONE

Heart wiped a raindrop from the tip of her nose.

She pulled her cloak tighter and shivered.

Davey's wagon was stuck fast.

Its wheels were half buried in mud.

Davey sat on the driver's bench.

The reins were loose in his hands. His jacket and shirt were dark with rainwater. His trousers were mud stained.

The horses were nervous and he was singing to them.

Heart brushed at her own clothes, then at Moonsilver's armor. The boots Josepha had given her were caked in mud. *Everything* was.

"We need a hand!" Binney was shouting. "Davey's stuck."

Groans rose from the long line of Gypsy wagons.

Heart made a face. Every muscle in her body was sore.

They had been struggling against the weather since they had left Bidenfast.

Usually, Binney said, they made it to Lord Kaybale's sheltered valleys before the worst storms hit. Not this year.

Winter in Lord Levin's mountains had been long and cruel.

They had spent months huddled in the crowded wagons.

The cold didn't seem to bother Moonsilver or Avamir. It was terrible for everyone else.

Zim had been sick for weeks, sniffling and coughing. The horses shivered and stood close together. Kip slept inside Binney's wagon, curled in a ball so tight his tail covered his ears.

The snow storms finally stopped.

Then the rains had begun.

The streams had turned into deep torrents of dark, muddy water.

There was a low, distant rumble of thunder. "Not much chance we'll sleep dry tonight," Talia called. She pointed at the dark clouds overhead. "Looks like another storm."

Heart glanced up. "It has to clear up sometime."

Talia grinned. "The sooner the better."

Heart didn't answer. She was sick of the cold, of the wet, of the wagons being so crammed with people every evening that she couldn't read or practice writing.

Tibbs had left behind a whole packet of paper.

Heart had found a hawk's feather to make a quill pen.

She knew her writing wasn't very good yet.

She could barely read it.

But she was determined to improve.

"I miss our campfires," Talia said. "None of us has practiced reading since Tibbs left. Not even you."

Heart nodded unhappily. It was true.

She hadn't told the Gypsies about Moonsilver healing Lord Irmaedith, or the storybook he had given her, and only Zim knew about Lord

3

Dunraven's. So she had to keep them hidden.

She wanted to tell Binney everything.

But it was forbidden for commoners to have books. And one of the books in her carry-sack had been taken from Lord Dunraven's castle.

If she got caught, Heart didn't want the Gypsies to get into trouble too.

"Maybe Gypsies just aren't supposed to learn to read," Talia said.

Heart glanced at her. "Everyone should learn."

Talia laughed. "The Lords of the Lands surely don't agree with that. I wonder why."

"They don't want people to know the old stories," Heart said slowly. This was something she had thought about a lot. "They want to keep all kinds of things secret."

Talia arched her brows. "Why?"

Heart wasn't quite sure why, but she knew it was true.

"We're set!" Binney shouted.

Heart sighed.

Talia frowned.

Kip whined, a high-pitched, unhappy sound.

Heart leaned down to pat his head. "Stay here."

Slogging through the mud, Heart and Talia joined the line of people getting ready to help.

Binney and Zim had worked a rope around the back of the wagon.

Heart found a place between Talia and Josepha.

She wiped her hands on her cloak for a better grip.

On the opposite side of the mud mire another line was forming. They would hold the other end of the rope.

Four men pulled off their boots.

They rolled up their trousers.

Then they waded into the mud.

The men lined up shoulder to shoulder, their hands flat against the wagon gate.

"Ready?" Binney shouted.

Heart nodded along with everyone else.

Davey stood up on the footrest.

The horses leaned into their harness collars. They knew what to do.

"Ready?" Binney yelled. "One, two . . . THREE!"

"Pull!" Davey urged his horses. "PULL!"

Heart leaned backward, digging her boot heels into the muddy earth. She could hear people groaning with effort.

The men behind the wagon were bent almost double, their heads down as they strained to push.

"Yah!" Davey shouted at the horses. "You can do it!"

Heart heaved at the rope.

Her hands hurt. She pulled harder anyway.

Finally, a wet, squelching sound made her glance up. The wheels were coming free!

She gritted her teeth and pulled harder, along with everyone else.

The wagon lurched forward. Heart stumbled backward as the rope went slack. Talia staggered, trying to keep her balance.

Binney lifted her head. "Hurrah! There is no mud puddle too fierce for us!"

Heart heard quiet laughter on all sides.

"You are all heroes!" Binney raised her arms like

an acrobat landing a back flip. "You are the conquerors of mud and drizzle!"

The laughter came again. Heart smiled. Binney reminded her of Ruth Oakes. They would be good friends if ever they met.

Suddenly the bracelet on Heart's wrist tightened.

Startled, Heart pushed up her cloak to stare at the woven silver threads.

Sometimes it seemed like the bracelet tightened to warn her of danger.

But nothing was wrong. . . .

The woods were still, except for the sound of the falling rain.

The Gypsies were all smiling, trudging back to their wagons.

Avamir and Moonsilver were walking calmly toward her.

Kip trotted with them, his ears plastered flat with rainwater. Heart pulled her cloak close around her shoulders.

✦CHAPTER TWO

The next two days, it rained steadily. Then it thinned to a constant sprinkle again.

"Ah!" Binney called out one morning. "I smell hearth smoke! Hickory Creek is over that hill!" She reined in her horses and pointed.

The whole line of wagons stopped.

The Gypsies cheered.

Heart frowned.

She pulled her carry-sack higher onto her shoulder.

Once they passed through Hickory Creek, they would be on their way out of the mountains.

What if the castle was just a story? What if she never found her family?

Binney was grinning. "We'll stock up on food,

then be off down the mountains onto Lord Kaybale's sunny plains."

Then, for the first time in days, the pattering rain stopped. Surprised, laughing, the Gypsies cheered again.

Zim waved at Heart. "Shall we put Moonsilver in the wagon so you can walk with us?"

Heart shook her head.

The wagons skidded and slewed in the slick mud. It scared Moonsilver to be locked inside one.

Zim nodded. "We'll camp outside the village. There's an old barn there we always use."

"I'll join you there after dark," Heart said. "I want to go into town to ask questions."

Zim shook rainwater out of his cloak.

Heart looked down the road. "Castle Avamir has to be somewhere, Zim."

He reached out and touched her cheek. "It might just be a legend, Heart—a campfire tale."

"Like unicorns?" she teased.

Zim laughed aloud. "Come back in time for supper," he said.

Heart reached out to touch Avamir's neck. "Go with them. You'll get out of the rain much sooner."

The mare shook her sodden mane, flinging a spray of rainwater into the air.

Avamir breathed against Heart's cheek, then Moonsilver's. Then she turned and broke into a canter.

Kip whined. He knew exactly what was going on.

"Go ahead," Heart said. "Stay with Avamir."

Heart watched Kip tear down the road. She slowed her step. Moonsilver stayed with her. They let the wagons get way ahead of them. Soon the Gypsies were nearly out of sight.

Heart patted Moonsilver's shoulder. She was so grateful for Joseph Lequire's gift. It was a grand disguise. The silvery armor he had made covered Moonsilver's back and sides.

And it hid his horn.

He looked like a nobleman's horse, not a unicorn.

He could pass through any town and be safe now. So far it had worked perfectly.

Heart pushed back the hood of her cloak.

Beneath it she was still wearing Gypsy clothes.

Moonsilver's disguise was perfect.

Hers was not.

Heart had a little money from playing her flute. But villages and small towns didn't have tailor's shops.

There had been no real towns on the High Road. They hadn't seen anything bigger than a village since Bidenfast.

Bidenfast.

It made Heart shiver to remember how close they had come to getting caught there.

If the young Lord Irmaedith had been less kind . . .

If Lord Dunraven had noticed what had happened . . .

Heart shivered again.

Then she felt Moonsilver's warm breath on the back of her neck.

Heart smiled.

Sometimes it seemed as if he knew when she was troubled.

"I have to find Castle Avamir," she told him, slowing so he could walk beside her.

Moonsilver shook his mane.

His armor clanked.

Heart stopped, and Moonsilver began to graze on a patch of rain-soaked grass.

"Castle Avamir is mentioned in the storybook three times so far," she told Moonsilver. "But it's all nonsense. The book says it's higher than the clouds, deep in a valley, under the stars, and over the moon."

Moonsilver lifted his head to look at her.

"And it might not have anything to do with my family, anyway," she admitted. "But Ruth gave me the name Heart Avamir and . . ." She stopped because she couldn't make sense out of anything she had learned so far.

Moonsilver went back to grazing. He tore up huge mouthfuls of the tender green grass. Heart didn't rush him. The farther the Gypsies were from them, the better.

Finally Moonsilver lifted his head.

Heart started off, heading uphill again.

When they got to the top of the rise, she slowed. Hickory Creek wasn't very big. There was one muddy street lined with rough log buildings.

Heart frowned.

She wouldn't be able to buy good clothes here.

She wondered what the people at Castle Avamir would think of the way she was dressed.

Maybe Zim was right. Maybe Castle Avamir *was* a legend.

But the woman in Jordanville had scolded her when she had asked about the Royal House of Avamir.

"But it might be a coincidence Ruth named me Heart Avamir," Heart murmured to Moonsilver. "Maybe *I* don't have anything to do with Castle Avamir at all."

Moonsilver whuffled a soft breath through his nostrils.

Heart looked at him. "Ruth is the one who told me to give your mother part of my own name."

Heart blinked back tears.

She missed Ruth Oakes.

"Why didn't I ask Ruth where the name Avamir came from?" Heart asked the gray sky overhead. "Why didn't I even *wonder*?"

Moonsilver lifted his head sharply.

Heart turned to look down the road.

A flicker of motion caught her eye.

Halfway down the hill a girl in a long blue skirt was sitting on a fallen log. She wasn't looking toward Heart.

She was facing the other way, bent forward, her shoulders hunched up.

The silver bracelet around Heart's wrist tightened.

Heart caught her breath.

She dodged behind the trees beside the road.

+CHAPTER THREE

Heart's pulse was thudding. Was there some reason to be afraid of the girl?

The bracelet was loose again, but it had pinched her *hard*.

Moonsilver stood close beside Heart.

A breeze stirred the tree branches.

The rain started again, then stopped, then started once more.

This time, it poured.

Heart leaned forward, letting the rain drip off her hood.

Moonsilver stood with his head down.

He sidled closer, Heart using her cloak's hem to shelter his face from the downpour.

Heart turned the bracelet around and around on her wrist.

It was magic, she was sure. It had woven itself out of the silver threads Ruth and Binney had given her.

But what did it mean when it tightened?

The rain came down hard for a few minutes. Then it thinned again and stopped.

Moonsilver nudged Heart's arm.

He let out a long fluttering breath.

He pushed at her shoulder.

"All right, all right." Heart gave in. "The rain probably chased her home." She peeked out from behind her hiding place.

The girl was at the bottom of the long hill, walking down the main street. She was almost running, her head bowed.

As Heart watched, the girl disappeared into a building with a steeply shingled roof.

"She's gone," Heart said to Moonsilver.

He stamped a hoof.

"We'll just talk to one or two people, then we'll go find Binney and the others," Heart promised him.

Moonsilver lifted his head high.

He switched his tail.

Heart pulled the soft cotton halter from her cloak pocket. Moonsilver lowered his head.

He understood.

They had to pretend she was leading him so people would think he was an ordinary horse.

Heart held the lead rope tightly. They squished and slid their way down the muddy hill.

Halfway down, Heart saw the girl's footprints near the log she had been sitting on.

There was a single blue thread caught on the bark of the fallen tree.

Heart turned when a tiny glimpse of yellow caught her eye.

Something was sticking out from beneath the log.

Heart looked down the road, then back at the little patch of yellow.

Cloth?

Heart glanced up again.

There wasn't a single person on the main street of Hickory Creek.

She whispered to Moonsilver to stand still.

Then, pretending to rebutton her boot, Heart sat on the log.

She bent to touch the cloth. It was stiff with wax.

She tugged at the cloth gently.

A packet slid out from beneath the hollow log.

Heart picked up the small package. She took in a quick breath. It was a book. The girl had been reading!

But how had a girl in a tiny mountain village gotten a book? How had she learned to read?

Heart looked at the first few pages.

The words weren't simple. They were harder than the book young Lord Irmaedith had given her.

There were pictures in the book. The first one showed a man standing beside a unicorn.

Heart stared. There was a tiny child sitting on the unicorn's back.

Heart held the book closer.

The drawing was dark but it looked as if the child was wearing a strange cloak of some kind. The cloth billowed out as though the wind were blowing. It looked as if the child had wings.

A spatter of raindrops fell, and Heart snapped the book shut. She rewrapped the waxed cloth to protect the book. The sprinkle thickened into rain.

Heart pushed the book back into its hiding place and started down the long hill, walking fast.

Moonsilver caught up. He lowered his head until the halter rope touched her hand.

Heart grabbed it, feeling foolish. No matter how excited she was to find the girl or how much she wanted to talk to her, she couldn't forget that Moonsilver had to look like a horse to anyone who saw them.

There was a sign hanging over the door of the steep-roofed building.

It was carved from wood and showed a bowl of steaming soup and a loaf of bread.

"I'll hurry," Heart told Moonsilver.

She looped the rope over the hitching-rail.

Moonsilver shook his mane, his armor clanking like silver bells.

Heart stepped up onto a broad porch. Fire logs

had been stacked neatly on the rough planks.

She lifted the iron clapper and let it fall.

"Come in!" someone shouted from within.

Heart pushed the door open. Warmth surrounded her instantly. The room smelled like apples and vegetable soup.

"Good afternoon," a woman near the fire said. "Do you need provisions, or are you just wanting a place to dry out?"

Heart closed the door. "Both."

She looked around. Bags of apples were stacked along the back wall.

Baskets of washed turnips and carrots and sprouting yams had been piled beside them.

There were rounds of cheese in wooden casks.

Heart's mouth watered. "I would like a bag of apples and some cheese, please."

The woman brought her the food and took her coins.

Heart pulled in a deep breath. "May I ask you something?"

The woman looked up. "What?"

Just then, a side door opened and the girl in the long blue skirt came in.

"Laura!" the woman said, turning to scowl at her. "Where have you been?"

"Just doing my work," the girl answered meekly. She smiled timidly at Heart.

Heart looked into her eyes.

Books were forbidden to common people in most of the lands. And this girl had hidden hers very carefully.

So her mother almost certainly didn't know about it.

Maybe no one did.

Heart wanted to talk to the girl alone, but she knew she might not get the chance. So she asked the question she had been asking everywhere she went.

"Do you know Castle Avamir?"

The woman shook her head. "Never heard of it."

Heart glanced the girl.

Laura's eyes were wide and her skin had gone as pale as milk.

✦CHAPTER FOUR

"Get firewood, Laura," the woman said.

The girl glanced at Heart, then went out the front door, dragging her feet.

Heart turned. "Thank you," she said quickly. "The apples look very good." The woman did not smile.

Heart swung her carry-sack over her shoulder and hurried out.

Laura was standing beside the pile of hearth logs. She was staring at Moonsilver. "He looks like a unicorn with that armor," she whispered.

Heart bit her lip.

Laura smiled timidly. "I love the old campfire stories."

Heart nodded cautiously. "So do I."

Laura's smile was wistful, dreamy. "There were rumors last summer. People said that a unicorn was seen in Dunraven's lands."

Heart blinked.

Of course.

The rumors about Moonsilver had spread in all directions—and she had traveled in a wide circle with the Gypsies. If Binney stayed on the usual route, they'd be back in Dunraven's lands by spring.

"You've heard of Castle Avamir, haven't you?" Heart asked quickly.

The girl nodded, the barest movement of her head. Her eyes flicked to the shop door, then back to Heart's face.

Heart moved closer. "Do you know where it is? Did you read something about it? I saw your book and—"

The girl's frightened gasp made Heart stop.

"I was very careful with it. I looked at a few pages, then I put it back in your hiding place," Heart said. "I won't tell anyone."

Laura took a step backward.

Heart understood. Laura thought she was a lord's stable page. She was afraid.

"Please," Heart begged. "I won't tell. But I have to find the castle. My family is there."

Laura was trembling.

Heart touched her arm. "I won't tell. I promise."

Laura took a deep breath. "Summer before last," she whispered, "there were two girls hiding in the woods, Leah and Terrin. I took food to them."

She paused, and Heart waited, glancing at the shop door.

"They were so hungry," Laura said softly. Then she looked up. "They showed me the storybook. They even read two of the stories to me. It was like magic—the words on the paper—but then"— Laura's eyes closed—"then one day they were gone."

Heart glanced at the door again. "Did they say anything about Castle Avamir?"

"Only that they lived there," Laura whispered.

Heart felt her pulse pounding. "Why were they hiding?"

Laura leaned in close. "They were afraid of Lord Dunraven."

Heart felt cold prickling on the back of her neck. "Dunraven? Here in Lord Levin's lands?"

"That's what they said," Laura told her.

Heart clenched her fists. "Where is the castle?"

Laura hesitated. "I asked them that."

Heart felt disappointment settle onto her shoulders. "They wouldn't tell you?"

Laura smiled timidly. "Nothing that made sense."

"Tell me," Heart pleaded.

Laura closed her eyes to recite the words. "Home lies higher than the clouds, deep in a valley, under the stars, and over the moon."

Heart caught her breath. "Thank you!"

Laura was shaking her head. "But it doesn't make sense."

Heart smiled. It *didn't*. But if the girls had said the same thing the book said . . . maybe it was true.

"Promise you won't tell anyone about the book?" Laura said. Her eyes were full of worry. "Most of the girls already think I am strange and—"

"You have my word of honor," Heart said quickly. "Will you do me a favor?"

Laura nodded. "If I can."

Heart knew that if she went to get Kip and Avamir, she would have to explain to Binney where she was going.

Heart drew in a long full breath.

The Gypsies would try to stop her—or they would insist on coming with her.

Heart knew she couldn't allow that. If Dunraven was involved, her journey would be dangerous.

She looked at Laura. "There is a old barn outside of town, where the Gypsies stay and—"

"I know it," Laura interrupted. "I take vegetables to the shoemaker's wife down that road every evening."

Heart smiled. "Good. Your mother won't get angry, then. Tell the Gypsies I'll see them soon. Just that. Nothing else."

Laura put her hand on her heart. "I will. And if you find Leah and Terrin, tell them I miss them?"

Heart smiled. "I promise."

"I wish you lived here," Laura said quietly. She ducked her head, studying her muddy feet. "I don't have any friends."

Heart felt the bracelet tighten again.

"She isn't my mother," Laura said suddenly, tipping her head toward the door.

Heart rubbed the bracelet through her cloak. "She isn't?"

Laura shook her head. "She says she found me asleep in the turnip patch."

The shop door suddenly banged open. "Get that firewood in here!"

Laura's eyes went wide, like a startled fawn.

"Stop your idling!" the woman scolded. "Get inside!"

Laura whirled and ran back through the door.

The woman turned and slammed it shut behind them.

Heart blinked.

There were so many questions she wanted to ask Laura.

Moonsilver pawed at the mud.

Heart turned to face him.

"There'll be no dry bed for us tonight," she told Moonsilver.

He shook his head, making his armor clank.

"I really don't know which way to go," Heart admitted. "But I have to try to find Castle Avamir. Your mother and Kip are safe with the Gypsies."

Moonsilver nuzzled Heart's shoulder.

He turned, pulling the loose lead rope with him.

Then he started off, dragging it in the mud.

Heart ran to catch up.

She grabbed the lead rope and lengthened her stride so it would look like she was leading him, and not the other way around.

✦CHAPTER FIVE

At the top of the muddy hill, Heart turned in a slow circle.

There was a bank of clouds on the western horizon.

Only one peak jutted above them.

"'Higher than the clouds,'" Heart said to herself.

She left the road and set off through the forest.

She walked westward—straight toward the lowering sun.

The trees were thick in the valleys, and Heart and Moonsilver had to wade through creeks.

With every step, Heart got more excited.

What would it be like to find her family at last?

Maybe the girls Laura had found were her cousins! Heart caught her breath. Maybe she had sisters!

The woods were quiet except for the gentle off-and-on sprinkle of rain.

There were no houses, no roads, no people.

Once they were well away from Hickory Creek, Heart laid the halter rope over Moonsilver's neck.

They had no need to pretend when they were alone.

Like Avamir always had, Moonsilver matched his stride to Heart's.

Heart kept walking. She was careful to follow paths made by deer and rabbits. The animals knew the easiest way through the mountains.

The drizzle finally stopped at sunset. Heart found a copse of hickory trees so thick the rain had barely come through.

The ground wasn't dry, but it wasn't too wet.

Heart took off Moonsilver's armor.

He shook himself, then rubbed his cheek against a tree trunk. He cantered in a circle, tossing his head. Heart wished she could stand the chill like he could.

She shivered.

Then she gathered a few fallen branches.

She propped them against a low limb.

Using twine from her carry-sack, Heart tied the armor plates into place, making a roof for shelter.

Then she built a small fire beneath it.

The warmth was wonderful.

She dried her cloak.

She gave Moonsilver four apples. He ate them one after another, crunching the sweet fruit.

Then he went to graze.

Heart ate an apple, then a little of the cheese. She yawned and looked up at the dimming sky.

She remembered her first days in Lord Dunraven's forest.

She had been so scared.

Every little sound had made her nervous.

Now she loved to sleep beneath an open sky.

Overhead the clouds were clearing off.

Heart set about making a bed of leaves. She found the driest ones she could and piled them high.

The warmth of the fire began to dry them.

By the time she lay down, they were warm and no longer wet.

Moonsilver settled close beside her.

He reached out and touched her cheek with his muzzle, then lowered his head to sleep.

Heart stared at the stars for a long time before she closed her eyes.

The next morning, Heart rose with the sun.

Moonsilver was already grazing in the clearing.

He cantered toward her.

In minutes his armor was back in place.

Heart fastened the straps, buckling them smoothly and quickly.

"'Higher than the clouds, deep in a valley, under the stars, and over the moon,'" Heart said to herself as they began walking.

From the valley she was in, Heart couldn't see the mountain peak.

It didn't matter.

She headed away from the sunrise.

That meant she was still traveling westward. She

would see the mountain peak as soon as they were high enough again.

The sun rose as she walked.

She stopped to marvel at the blue sky and wished she could be with Binney and the others.

They would celebrate such a beautiful day. There would be laughter and singing, and Zim would play his flute.

Heart blinked back tears. Why couldn't she ever stay with the people she loved?

Heart wiped her eyes.

It had been nearly a year since she had seen Ruth Oakes.

Moonsilver had been a young colt when they had run away from Ash Grove.

Thinking about Ash Grove made Heart think about Tibbs Renner.

And Simon.

Heart pulled her flute out of her carry-sack.

She played softly to quiet her thoughts.

Coming around a bend in the path, she noticed a thick stand of maple trees.

As she passed beneath them, she saw that their long branches had grown into a tangle overhead.

It was like standing beneath a single, giant tree.

Heart heard something rustling in the leaves.

She looked upward.

The sound stopped.

"Squirrels," she said to Moonsilver.

But Moonsilver was twisting his long neck to look up into the branches.

His eyes were rimmed in white and his tail was arched.

He sidestepped, lifting his hooves high.

Heart touched his shoulder.

He was trembling.

Then, suddenly, he lowered his head and nudged her. Heart nearly stumbled.

She stopped, trying to see up into the branches.

Moonsilver nudged her again. He drew a quick, startled breath. "What are you afraid of?" Heart asked him in a low voice.

He switched his tail and snorted, pushing at her shoulder.

"All right," Heart said. "We'll go."

She started walking, taking long strides. Once they were in a clearing, beneath the open sky, she glanced back at the maple trees.

They looked like ordinary maples, except for the strange, knotted branches.

Moonsilver blew out a long, quavering breath.

He had stopped trembling, but Heart could tell he still was uneasy.

"You're probably a little scared without Avamir," Heart said quietly. "You've never been away from your mother."

Moonsilver stamped his forehoof.

Heart started walking, one hand on his neck. "Without Avamir, you're scared of squirrels in trees," she teased him. She glanced back toward the trees and saw a flash of lavender wings. "And songbirds!"

Moonsilver shook his head so hard his armor rattled.

Heart laughed.

He dropped his head and walked faster.

Heart had to run a few steps to catch up.

"I'm sorry," she said, feeling a little silly.

She talked to the unicorns all the time, and they seemed to understand her. But . . . was Moonsilver upset about her teasing?

His head was high and he was walking fast. It *looked* like he was ignoring her.

"I really am sorry," Heart insisted.

Moonsilver stopped. His ears were pricked forward. He was staring at something.

Heart looked up.

There was another stand of knotted maple trees in front of them.

"It was just birds!" Heart told him. She nudged his shoulder.

Moonsilver refused to go forward.

✦CHAPTER SIX

Heart tried pulling on the lead rope.

He would not move.

Then, abruptly, he walked forward by himself, veering to one side to go *around* the maple trees.

But Heart was still holding onto the rope.

She tried digging her heels into the wet earth, but it made no difference. Moonsilver dragged her along.

"Stop!" she demanded.

Moonsilver shook his mane and switched his tail.

He pulled her around the trees, then past them. Then he began to trot.

Heart managed to keep up at first, running alongside him.

Moonsilver did not slow his pace. Heart staggered along, holding the rope. Then he tossed his head, jerking it free.

Heart stumbled to a halt. "Moonsilver?" She wiped her sleeve across her face. "Moonsilver!"

He left the path and headed up the steep slope.

Heart ran after him.

She had no idea what to do. Moonsilver had never acted this way before.

"Where are you going?" she called to him. He slowed to a walk, but he didn't stop.

He turned to look back at her. Heart didn't feel silly talking to him anymore. She was too worried.

"I have to figure out what the book meant," Heart called out to him, desperately trying to think of some reason for him to come back to her. "We don't know where to go yet."

Moonsilver shook his mane. Heart lengthened her steps. She cupped her hands around her mouth. "Wait! I'm sorry I teased you!"

Moonsilver kept going.

Heart hitched her carry-sack higher onto her shoulder. She hoped they weren't near a town.

People would notice a girl chasing an armored horse.

They would think she was a careless stable page—that she had lost her lord's fancy battle mount.

Then they would try to catch him, hoping for a reward.

"Moonsilver!" Heart called.

He still didn't stop.

He didn't even slow down.

In fact he broke back into a trot.

His head was high, his tail flaring out on the breeze.

Heart was scared.

What would she do if he began to gallop? She couldn't possibly keep up with him. If he galloped out of sight, she could lose him altogether.

Would he do that? Would he run away?

"Moonsilver!" Heart sprinted, desperate to stay close.

She was terrified now. What would happen when someone saw Moonsilver running loose in the woods, all alone, without a page in sight?

His armor looked valuable.

Any villager would try to catch him.

And anyone who caught him would discover the truth.

Or, worst of all, some lord's hunters might decide to run him down.

Heart cried out. It was loud, a sound without words, her voice ragged with worry and fear.

Moonsilver slowed, then stopped.

Heart ran toward him.

He stood still, his head high, switching his tail uneasily.

Heart tried to stay calm, slowing down as she got closer.

Moonsilver was tall and beautiful and he looked grown up.

But he wasn't.

He needed her to be kind to him when he was scared. And he needed her to protect him.

"Moonsilver!" Heart said softly as she came up beside him.

She reached out for the rope, knowing that if he wanted to, he could jerk it from her hand again and gallop away.

Instead he reached out to nuzzle her cheek.

Heart was so relieved, her eyes stung with tears.

Moonsilver held still, letting Heart lean against his shoulder.

He shook his mane and looked at her steadily for a long moment. Then he did something Avamir had done only once, long ago.

He bent one foreleg.

At first, Heart thought he was doing his bowing trick, the one he used in the Gypsy shows.

Then Moonsilver put his weight on his bent knee. He was kneeling, looking at her.

"Ride?" Heart whispered. "Why?"

Moonsilver fluttered a long breath out of his nostrils. Heart ached to know what he was trying to tell her.

"Are we in danger?" she said, breathlessly.

He tossed his head and flattened his ears against his neck.

Then he lowered his head, staring at her from beneath his long white eyelashes.

Awkwardly holding her carry-sack, Heart scrambled onto Moonsilver's back.

The plates of armor were cold against her legs, but the smooth metal didn't hurt.

Moonsilver stood.

Heart hung on.

She settled her carry-sack in front of her and tangled her fingers in his mane.

The moment she was ready, Moonsilver reared, then lunged forward, breaking into a gallop.

Heart clung tightly to his mane.

✦CHAPTER SEVEN

It began to rain again.

Moonsilver galloped through the woods, leaping fallen logs and jumping creeks. He stopped only long enough for them to sleep.

At the end of four wet, miserable days, they had traveled farther than Heart could have walked in a fortnight.

On the fifth morning, Moonsilver didn't kneel.

He stood patiently while Heart broke camp.

When she was ready, he led the way. He walked slowly enough that she could keep up.

Heart was glad he hadn't knelt again.

Her legs and back were sore from riding, and it felt very odd to ride Moonsilver, even if it had been his idea.

At noon, they topped a ridge.

Through the sprinkling rain, Heart saw the mountain peak again.

It had looked big from a distance.

Up close, it seemed to fill half the world.

Heart walked slowly as they started upward.

"'Under the stars and over the moon,'" she whispered to herself. It had to mean something. But what?

They came upon the road at noon.

She barely noticed it at first.

It wasn't a very wide road.

It was rough.

There were no wagon tracks, and the hoofprints in the soil were old, blurred by rain.

Not many used this road. And no one had come down it in a long time.

Still, Heart was uneasy.

Roads led to towns.

Towns meant that people were nearby—and that meant Moonsilver might be in danger.

Heart walked beside him, taking his lead rope

and pretending to guide him along.

But he was walking faster now, pulling *her* instead.

He broke into a prancing trot. "Slow down," Heart said, but Moonsilver didn't respond.

He trotted a little faster.

Heart clung to the lead rope. If he ran away from her again . . .

Heart caught at Moonsilver's mane. "Slow down! We can't just follow a road like this!"

Moonsilver stopped and looked at her.

"We have to be careful," Heart told him, hoping he could understand. "What if some townsman tries to catch you?"

Moonsilver tossed his head. Heart could tell what he was thinking. He was sure no one *could* catch him.

Heart frowned. "The storybooks say that lordsmen once hunted unicorns. Even if they can't catch you, they might—"

Moonsilver jerked his head up, his ears tipped forward.

An instant later, Heart heard it too. Someone was singing.

She dragged at the lead rope. Moonsilver followed her off the road.

Together they hid behind a stand of birches. Heart hoped the white bark would blend with Moonsilver's coat.

She laid one hand on Moonsilver's muzzle.

Above them on the road, a man came into sight.

He had a cloak, but no hood or hat.

He was walking slowly, his shoulders hunched up as though he was trying to keep his ears warm in the gentle rain.

Heart peeked out to watch him pass.

He was still singing; the song was timed to his steps.

He looked old.

He tapped at the ground with a long walking stick.

There was a heavy carry-sack on his back, and his trousers were stained the color of the earth. A

farmer? He was probably carrying vegetables to trade in town.

Moonsilver blew out a long breath.

Heart turned to look at him. "There must be a village up ahead."

Moonsilver shook his mane.

Heart held the lead rope tightly.

She wanted to find the village.

She wanted to ask people if they knew anything about Castle Avamir.

But now she was worried. "Will you stay close to me?" she asked Moonsilver.

He shook his mane, then touched her cheek with his velvety muzzle.

"You have to," Heart said. "You have to pretend to be a horse if we are going to be among people."

Moonsilver looked at her steadily. Heart wished for the thousandth time that they could just *talk*, that she could be sure they understood each other.

Heart gripped the rope as they climbed back up the slope, but Moonsilver went slowly, keeping pace with her.

Once they were on the road again, Heart walked faster.

Rounding the first bend, she expected to see the old man in front of them. But he wasn't there.

He had turned off someplace, but where? He was probably a woodcutter, living alone in the forest.

The road curved in wide turns, winding upward.

It got steeper. . . .

Much steeper.

Heart kept walking.

After a long time, the sprinkling rain stopped. She pushed back her hood, then raised it again.

The forest was still thick with fog. It chilled her skin and tickled her nose.

Heart shivered and walked on. Moonsilver stayed close at her side, and she was grateful.

The road was so steep in places, that Heart had to stop to catch her breath. Twice she considered turning around, but she didn't. All roads led *somewhere.*

After a time, finally, the clinging mist thinned.

Heart stopped to rest and turned to look down the mountainside.

There was a thick bank of the milky fog below her.

At that instant the sun broke through and startled her into looking up.

The sky overhead was blue. For the first time in months, there wasn't a cloud anywhere—no sign of a storm near or far.

It had been stormy for so long!

Heart looked back down the slope, then glanced upward again. Suddenly she understood.

The clouds hadn't disappeared or even thinned. She had just climbed *through* them.

Heart smiled. She was above the clouds!

She started upward again, excited.

She half-expected to see a shining castle at every turn.

But every curve in the road brought more trees, more meadows, an endless green landscape.

The forest thinned as she got higher, but it seemed to go on forever.

The hours passed and she began to get discouraged again.

Maybe the book was only nonsense after all.

Maybe Laura's friends had just been some nobleman's daughters playing at running away from home. Maybe they had tricked Laura, making up stories to entertain her so she'd keep bringing them food.

Heart kicked at the dirt. And maybe she was a hundred days' travel from Castle Avamir and was heading in the wrong direction.

Or maybe it didn't exist at all.

Heart kept going until the sun began to sink into the clouds below.

Only then did she turn off the road.

Her legs ached from climbing all day.

So she chose the downhill side.

✦CHAPTER EIGHT

The land fell away more steeply than Heart had thought it would.

She skidded and slid, looking for a stand of trees thick enough to hide them for the night.

Moonsilver danced his way down the slope, crossing rocky ground no horse could have managed.

The land finally leveled out.

Heart spotted a dense grove of ash trees and smiled.

The evening light was getting dim.

They made their way into the trees.

Heart was surprised to come upon a wide meadow and a clear, deep lake.

Heart squinted, trying to see in the gathering dusk.

Past the lake, it looked like the land rose again in rocky ledges, sharp and forbidding.

Heart glanced at Moonsilver.

He stood looking out over the water.

Heart took Moonsilver's armor off and stacked the pieces carefully.

She made a tiny fire and warmed herself while he grazed.

She ate cheese and apples.

She made a bed of leaves.

They both drank cold, clean water from the lake.

Heart lay down for the night.

Moonsilver settled in nearby. His breathing slowed and steadied.

Heart was tired.

She felt herself sinking into sleep.

For the first time in a long time, her old dreams returned.

She was running.

The earth and the rocky ground were the color of the moon.

Then, near dawn, she awoke.

It took a moment to slow her breath, to understand that she wasn't running—she had been dreaming.

She stared upward. The stars glittered in the cloudless sky. After months of storms, she was thrilled to watch the moon rise.

It was full, a pale yellow circle floating in the darkness.

Heart slid from beneath her blanket and stood up.

The steep-sided valley had been touched by moonlight.

It turned Moonsilver's coat from white to silver, like the night he had been born.

It transformed the lake into a mirror.

Heart stared into the still water.

Then she pulled in a quick breath and shivered.

"Home lies 'higher than the clouds, deep in a valley, under the stars, and over the moon,'" Heart whispered to herself.

She had climbed through the clouds, and was higher than the rainstorms now.

Then, when she had left the road, she had come downhill into this deep valley.

Now the stars were out overhead.

And *below* her the moon shone in the mirror of the still lake.

Heart felt her bracelet tighten.

She reached down to touch it, her breath coming quickly.

If the words from her book were true, Castle Avamir had to be somewhere among the rocky ledges she had seen in the dusk.

Heart looked down the slope.

The sunrise was below the clouds.

It was lighting the mist in golds and pinks.

Heart turned to see Moonsilver waking, stretching out his forelegs.

He stood up and faced her.

"It has to be up there," Heart said, pointing. "Castle Avamir. It has to be."

He tossed his head, pranced in a wide circle as she washed her hands and face in the lake.

She raked her fingers through Moonsilver's mane, then rebraided her own hair.

She put Moonsilver's armor on slowly.

The sun burst above the clouds.

Heart looked across the lake.

The slope below the ledges was covered in maple trees.

She looked into Moonsilver's eyes.

"Don't get scared of songbirds again. Stay close to me. If my family is up there . . ."

Heart trailed off. She wasn't sure what she had meant to say.

She was shivering with cold and excitement.

Would her family really be there?

What would her mother look like?

Moonsilver shook his mane.

He pawed at the ground.

Heart slid the halter over his ears. She gripped the lead rope. "Stay close," she whispered. She could feel her pulse.

She squared her shoulders.

Then she picked up her carry-sack and began to walk.

Moonsilver was uneasy beneath the maple trees.

He kept tossing his head. But he did not stop.

Heart clung to the rope.

The shade of the trees was so deep, so dark, that she could not see very far ahead.

So the appearance of the first wall of gray stone surprised her.

Moonsilver stopped in front of it. Heart looked up.

It was higher than any wall she had ever seen—higher than Lord Irmaedith's castle in Bidenfast, higher than Dunraven's castle.

The maple branches grew toward the wall, then angled straight up, seeking sunlight.

Heart followed the wall, touching it timidly with her fingertips.

When the wall changed directions she walked along it, heading uphill.

The gates were at the top of the slope.

They hung on massive iron hinges.

The wood was black, and as thick as a tree trunk.

It had been carved.

Heart stared. The design was the same as the one on her baby blanket. It matched the gates on

the library in Jordanville, and the drawing in Tibbs's book. The original iron gates—the ones that had been made by Joseph Lequire's great grandfather—had to be inside these walls.

This *was* Castle Avamir. . . .

"Who is there?"

The sudden shout made Heart jump.

Moonsilver snorted in a sharp breath and reared.

Heart stood still, clinging to the rope.

"Heart Avamir," she called back, then cleared her throat and called her name out a second time, a little louder.

She was trembling as she waited for the voice to come again.

But instead there was a high creaking sound.

The massive gates swung inward.

Moonsilver turned to look back at the trees. Heart pulled his head round. "Stay close," she whispered.

Then she went forward.

She stood up straight, keeping her shoulders squared.

She expected to see people walking along the

castle parapets. She expected the voices of children and the sounds of horses and hens and cows.

But the courtyard was empty.

The castle was silent.

It was beautiful.

The spires soared high.

The walls enclosed a garden.

Heart walked toward it.

There was a lilac hedge taller than a man.

There were trimmed boxwoods, cedars, and flowers of every color. A bed of deep red roses was in full bloom.

Heart was puzzled. Outside the walls, winter had barely ended.

The roses' perfume mixed with the sweet scent of lavender and lilac, layered in with the cool dawn air.

"Why have you come back?" the voice asked.

Heart spun around.

It was the old man who had passed them on the road.

Standing this close to him, she could see that his eyes were milky and unfocused. Was he blind?

He leaned on his walking stick.

"I am looking for my family and I—," Heart began.

The old man chuckled, interrupting her. "No one's family dares to live here anymore." He bent to cut a strange-looking flower.

Heart glanced around.

The garden was perfectly kept. But beyond it, the castle was still.

There was no smell of morning cookfires, no hint of people. She caught a glimpse of purplish wings flashing into an open window.

"Where did they all go?" Heart whispered. Her throat was tight.

"I don't know," the man said quietly.

He straightened and began to walk toward her. His steps were sure. If he was blind, he knew the garden very well. "For a long time, they put their little ones out for others to find," the man said quietly.

"Put out for others to find."

Heart thought about Laura.

She thought about herself—about how Simon had found her in the tall grass by the Blue River.

"Why?" she asked, breathlessly. Then she cleared her throat. "Why would they do that?"

The old man tipped his head. "To save you, of course."

Heart shook her head. "Save us? From what?"

The man came toward her, extending the flower.

Heart took it, staring into his odd, clouded eyes.

He smiled. "A homecoming gift, the only one I can give you."

Heart was trembling. "Don't you know where they are?"

Before the man could answer, Moonsilver nudged at her shoulder. A second later, she heard what he had heard.

Hoofbeats.

The old man lifted his head. "Hide," he commanded.

Heart whirled around in a circle. She couldn't go out the gate. The sound of galloping horses was too close.

She ran, leading Moonsilver into the garden, around to the far side of the lilac hedge.

Moonsilver lay down.

Heart crouched beside him.

She saw the old man running toward the gates. He grabbed a thick rope and pulled. But it was too late.

"Good morning, gardener," a rasping voice called out.

Heart recognized it instantly.

It made her skin prickle and tighten.

Lord Dunraven!

The girls had told Laura the truth, then.

Heart pressed her lips together. She could hear her own heartbeat.

If Lord Dunraven found her now, if he saw the book she had taken from his castle . . . and if he found out about Moonsilver . . .

"Get your things, old man," Dunraven said in his rough-edged voice.

Heart peeked out from her hiding place.

The old man was shaking his head. But Lord Dunraven and his men were circling around him.

"Your queen calls for you," Dunraven said in an ugly, mocking voice.

Moonsilver struck the earth with one hoof, and one of the guards glanced around.

Heart ducked down.

Moonsilver pressed close to Heart, and she could feel him trembling.

She put an arm around his neck.

If he made a sound now . . . they would be caught.

"Be still," Heart whispered into Moonsilver's ear. "They can't see us. We're safe."

She didn't believe them herself, but her words seemed to calm Moonsilver a little.

Just then the clattering of hooves began again.

Heart leaned forward to see through the hedge.

One of Dunraven's men had pulled the old man up behind his saddle.

They were galloping away.

Heart held her breath.

The sound of hoofbeats dimmed, then faded away.

Heart's bracelet tightened, then seemed to turn in a circle around her wrist.

Astonished, she shoved up her sleeve.

The flower in her hand seemed to leap free, spinning and changing, the bloom turning silver as it shrank.

Heart watched, breathing hard.

The long stem was a silver thread now, weaving itself into the silvery lace of her bracelet.

It was all over in an instant.

The silver flower, tiny and delicate, lay at the center of the bracelet.

The band of silver lace circled her wrist.

Heart could only stare.

Moonsilver stood beside her.

Above them, the silent castle stood high and proud—and empty.

Finally Heart looked up. "We have to follow them."

Moonsilver was glancing nervously at the maple trees just beyond the gate.

Heart understood. She was afraid, too—not of

the maple trees, but of everything that lay beyond them.

But that didn't matter.

There was only one thing she could do.

Moonsilver was kneeling down, and she kissed his silken cheek for understanding.

She scrambled onto his back.

She had found her home. Now she had to find her family—and save them if she could.

A r e   Y o u
Ready-for-Chapters

**Page-turning step-up books for kids ready to tackle
something more challenging than beginning readers**

The Cobble Street Cousins
by Cynthia Rylant
illustrated by
Wendy Anderson Halperin
#1 In Aunt Lucy's Kitchen
0-689-81708-8
#2 A Little Shopping
0-689-81709-6
#3 Special Gifts
0-689-81715-0

The Werewolf Club
by Daniel Pinkwater
illustrated by Jill Pinkwater
#1 The Magic Pretzel
0-689-83790-9
#2 The Lunchroom of Doom
0-689-83845-X

Third-Grade Detectives
by George Edward Stanley
illustrated by
Salvatore Murdocca
**#1 The Clue of the Left-
Handed Envelope**
0-689-82194-8
**#2 The Puzzle of the Pretty
Pink Handkerchief**
0-689-82232-4

Annabel the Actress
by Ellen Conford
illustrated by
Renee W. Andriani
0-689-83883-2

The Courage of Sarah
Noble
by Alice Dalgliesh
0-689-71540-4
$4.99/$6.99 Canadian

The Bears on Hemlock
Mountain
by Alice Dalgliesh
0-689-71604-4
$4.99/$6.99 Canadian

THE UNICORN'S SECRET

Experience the Magic

When the battered mare Heart Trilby takes in presents her with a silvery white foal, Heart's life is transformed into one of danger, wonder, and miracles beyond her wildest imaginings. Read about Heart's thrilling quest in

ALADDIN PAPERBACKS
Simon & Schuster Children's Publishing Division • www.SimonSaysKids.com

Ready-for-Chapters